The Bee Tree

Patricia Polacco

Philomel Books   New York

Copyright © 1993 by Patricia Polacco
Published by Philomel Books, a division of The Putnam & Grosset
Group, 200 Madison Avenue, New York, NY 10016.
All rights reserved. This book, or parts thereof, may not be
reproduced in any form without permission in
writing from the publisher.
Published simultaneously in Canada.
Book design by Colleen Flis.
The text is set in Cloister.

Library of Congress Cataloging-in-Publication Data
Polacco, Patricia. The bee tree / Patricia Polacco. p. cm.
Summary: To teach his granddaughter the value of books,
a grandfather leads a growing crowd in search of the tree
where the bees keep all their honey.
[1. Books and reading—Fiction. 2. Bees—Fiction.] I. Title.
PZ7.P75186Be   1993   92-8660 CIP AC [E]—dc20
ISBN 0-399-21965-X

1 3 5 7 9 10 8 6 4 2
First Impression

For Mary Ellen, my mother, who went on
to become a teacher for thirty-seven years...
and for her childhood friends,
Ole, Einar and Mary Agnes Tundevold,
with such love!

"I'm tired of reading, Grampa." Mary Ellen sighed. "I'd rather be outdoors running and playing."

"So you don't feel like reading, eh? Feel like running, do you? Then I expect this is just the right time to find a bee tree!" he said, taking down a jar and putting on his lucky hat.

"What's a bee tree, Grampa?" Mary Ellen asked.

"Well…it's where the bees make their home. It's where they keep the honey…the sweetest in the land!" Grampa chirped excitedly.

"But we already have honey, Grampa," Mary Ellen said.

"Ah, but not honey like this," her grampa answered with a wink.

Mary Ellen and her grampa put on their coats and went outdoors. They walked down past the hollyhocks to the garden and found bees gathering pollen from the flowers. Her grampa carefully trapped some in the glass jar, making sure not to hurt them.

When he was sure that he had enough, he smiled and leaned close to Mary Ellen. "They'll take the pollen back to the hive to make it into honey, and we'll be right behind them."

Then he slowly loosened the lid of the jar and let one single bee escape. It stayed on the mouth of the jar for a moment, flew straight up, then buzzed toward the cornfield.

"Quick now, RUN!" Grampa called out as he began to chase the bee.

Just then, Mrs. Govlock from down the creek way was walking Baby Sylvester in his carriage. Mary Ellen and her grampa ran by them. "We're off to find a bee tree today!" Grampa shouted.

"I haven't done that since I was a girl!" Mrs. Govlock said excitedly. "May I come too?"

Grampa motioned her to follow, and the three of them were off and running. Baby Sylvester laughed out loud as his carriage bumped and bounced through the rows of corn. "Honk" went a goose as it waddled after them.

As they came from the cornfield and crossed Dietz Junction, Einar Tundevold came around the bend on his squeaky old bike. "Where are you all going in such a hurry?" he asked.

"A bee tree," Mary Ellen puffed as the foursome scurried by.

"Chasing a bee to its tree...this I would like to do also," he said as he stood up and pedaled faster. The wheels of his bike went *tweddle-tweddle-squeeeeeeek*. Their boots slapped the ground. The buggy pitched and swayed, and the goose honked as they ran after that bee.

The bee swooped down, stopped, held in midair, then circled past them and headed straight for the St. Joe River.

Olav Lundheigen, while strolling on the nearby shore with the charming Hermann sisters, Petra and Dorma, looked up and noticed the commotion coming toward them. "Where are you all going?" he called out.

"To a bee tree, we are going!" Einar Tundevold puffed as he pedaled by.

"Can we come too?" the two lovely ladies pleaded.

"Fast, you'll have to run," Einar said.

"We don't care, let's go!" the three shouted as they raced after him.

Slap, bump, honk, tweddle-tweddle-squeak fump! they all went as they sped down the road after that bee.

"Klondike" Bertha Fitchworth, just back from an expedition in the Yukon, had car trouble next to the road. She looked up just in time to see everybody running by. "You say you're after a bee tree?" she shrieked. "Zounds, that won't be easy, but eureka, what an adventure!" She sprinted along behind them.

The bee dipped and soared as it made its way out of sight.

But Grampa carefully let another out, and the chase was on again!

The noisy, merry bunch galloped up over Bird Talk Fellow Ridge, only to run smack dab into Feduciary Longdrop's herd of goats. The goats bleated and bucked as the people clambered through them.

"What ho?" Feduciary called out. "You're gonna scare me goats!"

"A bee tree!" a voice called back.

With that Feduciary tooted his flute, and he and his flock joined the chase. "Bounding billies, this will be great!" he said on a dead run.

Three traveling musicians looked up just in time to see a thundering stampede of goats, buggies, people and bikes coming straight for them!

"Why are they all running, Pa?" one of the boys asked his father.

"We're after that bee!" Grampa said, pointing at the small dot in the sky.

"It's leading us to a bee tree," Mary Ellen wailed as she streaked by them.

"C'mon along!" "Klondike" Bertha chortled as she huffed past.

Slap, bump, bleat, honk, tweddle-tweddle-squeak fump! they went as they ran. Hoofs clattered. Rows of corn were parted. Nothing really mattered but chasing that bee!

They ran through Greiner's Bluff and into Bishop's Meadow, around Dead Man's Tree and then to Bird Talk Hollow.

As they ran down the hollow, the bee took blinding speed and disappeared from their sight. They all stopped to catch their breath just in front of Dunks Woods.

Grampa handed the jar with the last bee in it to Mary Ellen, and she let it out.

Sure enough, it flew straight and low, right into Dunks Woods.

"It's the bee tree!" Grampa whispered. "That's where the honey will
be, but we'll need plenty of smoke."

Everyone set about to build a smoke fire from twigs and damp leaves. When the smoke had quieted the bees, Grampa balanced on Einar's bicycle and reached into the tree. As he pulled out small pieces of honeycomb, he dropped them into some of Baby Sylvester's spare clean diapers that "Klondike" Bertha was holding. Mary Ellen tied them into neat little bundles, and Mr. Lundheigen put them into the baby carriage. The musicians played merrily as the Hermann sisters danced.

Grampa invited everyone back to the house for baking powder
biscuits, fresh brewed tea and, of course, the honey!
There was music, dancing, tall tales and raucous laughter as they all
buzzed about the sweet adventure of that day.

Grampa took Mary Ellen inside away from the crowd. "Now, child, I am going to show you what my father showed me, and his father before him," he said quietly.

He spooned the honey onto the cover of one of her books. "Taste," he said, almost in a whisper.

Mary Ellen savored the honey on her book.

"There is such sweetness inside of that book too!" he said thoughtfully. "Such things…adventure, knowledge and wisdom. But these things do not come easily. You have to pursue them. Just like we ran after the bees to find their tree, so you must also chase these things through the pages of a book!"

Then he smiled and hugged her.

From that day on, Mary Ellen never again complained about her reading. She found it to be every bit as exciting as a wild chase through the Michigan countryside, and as sweet as the honey from a bee tree.